Disney

5-Minute Sleepy Time Stories

Disney PRESS

Los Angeles • New York

Contents

Ducky and Bunny's Big Plan

Every day was a new adventure for Bo Peep, Woody, and their friends. They traveled from town to town helping toys.

Bo had collected many useful items for this task, but her sticky hand was one of her favorites. It was very handy for getting around. With a whirl and a whip, she could fling the sticky hand high up in the air and zip from place to place.

But one day the sticky hand went missing! Bo rummaged through her skunkmobile. She found paperclips, rubber bands, a roll of tape—but no sticky hand.

"Nothing else seems to be missing," said Officer Giggle McDimples, peering into the skunkmobile.

"Where did you last see it?" asked Woody.

"I remember using it by the Star Adventurer booth," said Bo.

Ducky and Bunny raced over at the mention of their old game booth.

"Oh, we know the Star Adventurer booth well," said Bunny. Ducky scowled. "And the guy who runs it."

"Yeah, he's gotta know where it is," said Bunny. "He's always taking toys and putting them on his prize wall."

The plush toys would never forget the day the Star Adventurer booth employee stuck Buzz Lightyear on the prize wall, knocking them from the top-prize spot.

"Oh ho ho, do we have a plan for you!" said Ducky.

First, Ducky and Bunny explained, they would need a distraction. The skunkmobile, driven by Bo's sheep, Billy, Goat, and Gruff, was perfect for the job.

"That'll keep the balloon person busy," said Ducky.

"While we hop on a flight," added Bunny.

"Ding! Going up," Ducky sang.

Next, Ducky and Bunny said, they would survey the area for the sticky hand.

"From up above we can see the whole carnival," said Ducky.

"Yeah," said Bunny, pointing down below. "We even see some kid eating cotton candy at the top of the Ferris wheel."

"It's sticking to his hair and all over his chin," said Ducky, laughing and getting distracted.

"Uh . . . guys?" interrupted Woody.

5

Ducky and Bunny paused and frowned as they looked over at Woody.

"How will that help us find the missing sticky hand?" Woody asked.

"We. Are. Getting there," said Bunny.

"Next, we float toward the Star Adventurer booth," said Ducky.

"When the time is right, we pop the balloon. . . ."

"Plush rush!" they cheered.

"We scream, 'Give up the stick hand, you thief!'" Bunny said.

Ducky laughed and added, "Yeah, 'Hand it over, Game Boy, or we'll—'"

"I don't think so," said Bo, bringing them back to reality.

Bo and Giggle McDimples stood there shaking their heads. This was not a good idea, and everybody knew it. The "plush rush" would never work.

Ducky and Bunny shrugged. "Yeah, you're right," said Ducky. "No plush rush." But they had another plan.

"First, we leave a trail for the Star Adventurer guy to follow," explained Bunny.

"It leads into the fun house," said Ducky.

"And right into our trap," added Bunny with a giggle.

"We follow
him through the
twirling tube."
said Ducky.

"And into the
house of mirrors . . ."
said Bunny.

"We wait until he's lost inside the mirror maze," said Ducky. "He has no idea what's coming next!"

"We corner him!" shouted Bunny. "And give him our hypnotic stare down! Then—"

"Wait . . ." interrupted Duke Caboom

He rode over to Ducky and Bunny on his motorcycle. He had a question about this plan.

"You two really know how to hypnotize someone?" he asked. Ducky and Bunny looked deep into Duke's eyes and nodded.

"Whoa," said Duke with a gulp.

Bo smiled at the outrageous plan. "You know, it's really not that big of a deal. I can find another sticky hand."

Ducky and Bunny shook their heads. They were determined to present Bo with the perfect plan.

"Here's our one-hundred-percent-will-absolutely-work-impossible-to-fail plan!" shouted Ducky.

"Oh, yeah," said Bunny. "This is it."

Ducky and Bunny were proud of themselves. They knew they had the best idea this time. Once they were sure everyone was paying attention, Ducky took the lead telling the group their new plan.

"Step one. We climb into our time machine," he started.

"We go back," said Bunny.

"Waaaaay back," said Ducky. "To the days of dinosaurs and hot lava and—"

Giggle cleared her throat. "Uh . . . guys?"

She knew Ducky and Bunny were getting carried away again. But she had her own idea of how to complete this mission and retrieve the sticky hand.

"What!" shouted Ducky and Bunny, irritated by yet another interruption.

"I've cracked the case," Giggle announced.

The friends all looked to see where Giggle was pointing. It was the sticky hand . . . stuck to Bunny's back! It had been fixed to his fur the whole time.

"Caboom!" cheered Duke.

Bunny yelped as Bo peeled it from his fur.

Ducky looked over at Bunny. "Hm. How did that happen?" he said.
"I guess you weren't paying attention again."

Bunny frowned. "Or you put it there and you forgot."

"Why would I put a sticky hand on your back?" asked Ducky.

Ducky and Bunny continued to bicker as Bo swung the sticky hand
above her head, winding up for their next big adventure.

It Takes Two

"We did it!" Mowgli hollered.

He had just escaped from King Louie and the monkeys with his friends Baloo and Bagheera.

"It sure was a swinging good time," Baloo said.

Bagheera was less enthusiastic. "Next time, we need to stick to the plan! We're lucky to be alive.

"We need to find a safe place for the night," Bagheera said.
"King Louie may still be after Mowgli."

"Aw, loosen up!" Baloo said. "I can protect us. If we see any
of those mangy monkeys, I'll jab with my left, and I'll swing with
my right—"

"Oh, Baloo. We need to protect the boy. Think about it."

Mowgli sighed. He didn't need protecting. Why, with his brawn he could fight like a bear, and with his brains he could plan like a panther, if only they'd give him the chance!

Just then Mowgli heard something.

He stopped listening to Baloo and Bagheera and followed the noise. He walked through lots of trees and vines. But every time he got close, the noise would move away and he'd have to keep chasing it.

Then, suddenly, there was a rustling sound above his head . . . somewhere in the trees.

Mowgli looked around. He saw something jump onto a branch.

"Hello?" Mowgli called up to the tree. "Come out and play!"

A little flying squirrel poked its head out of the leaves.

Mowgli giggled as the flying squirrel glided above him and landed on another branch.

"I want to try that!" Mowgli shouted. He climbed a tree and grabbed a vine.

"Wheeee!"
PLUNK!
"Woooo!"
CRASH!

Finally, Mowgli got the hang of it. It felt like flying! He and the squirrel swept over the heads of Bagheera and Baloo.

Mowgli was having the time of his life, but his stomach started grumbling. "There are some bananas! Let's race!" he cried.

But Mowgli and his new friend didn't know how to cross the river. Mowgli looked at the vine he was holding and got an idea.

"Let's swing," Mowgli said.

"On the count of three: one, two, *three*!"

"Eeeeeep!" the squirrel said.

Mowgli and the squirrel glided right over the river. Mowgli held on to his vine as tightly as he could. The squirrel was winning the race, but Mowgli was having so much fun he didn't even notice.

Kaa the snake had been watching, and he happened to be a very good swimmer. He waited for his prey on the other side of the river.

"Oh, there'ssssss the Man-cub sssssswinging to me," Kaa said.

Then Kaa watched as Mowgli and the squirrel headed right into the water.

SPLASH!

Kaa slithered down from his tree, and his eyes grew wide. "Trussssst in me," the snake said. "Jusssst sssslide into my coils."

Mowgli and the squirrel grabbed on to Kaa, who pulled them up into the tree with him.

"Oh, look. A ssssquirrel," Kaa hissed. The squirrel's eyes focused on Kaa.

Using his brain, Mowgli realized if he didn't look into Kaa's eyes, then the snake could not make him go to sleep.

And with his brawn, Mowgli wrapped Kaa's tail around a stone and dropped it.

The snake fell from the tree. "Ssssome thanksss I get!" Kaa muttered.

"Mowgli!"

"Little Britches!"

Bagheera and Baloo stood across the river, shouting.

"I'm over here!" Mowgli hollered. "I used my brains and my brawn to save—"

"What? We can't hear you!" said Baloo.

Mowgli turned to
his squirrel friend.

"Let's meet again," Mowgli
said. "Maybe next time I'll try
gliding *without* the vine. . . ."

The squirrel flew away, high
above the ground.

"Well, maybe that's not such a
good idea," Mowgli added.

Mowgli made his way downriver, past the
waterfalls. Bagheera and Baloo followed him on
the other side. When it was finally safe to cross,
Mowgli swung—and swam—to his friends.

That night, as Mowgli drifted off to sleep, he heard his friends still arguing.

"He didn't look in Kaa's eyes," Bagheera said.

"He used a big rock to get rid of Kaa," Baloo argued.

Mowgli smiled. He fell asleep thinking about his adventure-filled day. He had used his brains *and* his brawn to save himself and rescue his new friend!

Family Game Night

The sun began to set as the castle bell rang over Arendelle, signaling the end of another day. Anna, Elsa, Kristoff, and Olaf had been looking forward to hearing that lovely sound for hours. Life had been very busy, but there was one thing they always made time for—family game night! They quickly wrapped up their day's work, eager to spend the evening together.

The friends gathered inside the castle, and Olaf immediately launched into a game of charades.

"I'll go first," he said. In a flash, the snowman had rearranged himself so he looked like a pig.

"How about we try a different game tonight?" said Anna.

Olaf was happy to try something new. "So what should we play?" he asked.

Elsa suggested playing *stiv heks* in the courtyard. "One person is it, and if you get tagged, you stand still, like a statue," she explained. "But if someone else touches you, you're free to run again."

Freeze tag under the stars sounded wonderful.

Kristoff, Anna, and Olaf raced around the courtyard. But just moments later, Elsa reached out and accidentally froze their feet in place. "Oops," she said. "I didn't mean to do that!"

Elsa thought maybe someone else should be it. Anna was happy to volunteer.

Anna tagged Kristoff, forcing him to stand still as a statue. When Olaf tried to release Kristoff, she tagged him, too!

Just as Anna was about to tag Elsa, Anna's slippers froze to the ground again. Elsa smiled, embarrassed. "Maybe we should try another game."

Anna eagerly suggested one of her favorite board games: chess. "We can play on teams!" she exclaimed.

As they played, Anna became more and more enthusiastic. She couldn't help interjecting when she saw Kristoff and Olaf make a move. Then she reached over and nudged their piece into an even better position.

Elsa pushed one of their rooks forward three spaces, and Anna flinched. Elsa pulled the rook back to its place, and Anna nodded in approval.

Before long, Anna was playing for both sides. Family game night had turned into "watch Anna play chess" night.

When she finally realized it, she looked up at them with a sheepish smile. "I guess I got carried away," she said. "This isn't working, either, is it?"

They turned to Kristoff. It was his turn to pick a game.

"I thought you'd never ask," he said with a big grin. "We're going to need some space." Kristoff led them to the ballroom. He explained a game he used to play with his troll family, called roots and treetops. "And it's not about winning or losing," he added.

"Nobody loses," Kristoff
continued. "Everybody wins!"
The game required creativity,
balance, and coordination.
They tried and tried to follow
Kristoff's instructions, but
they toppled down each
and every time.

Kristoff could see his game was not working, either.

"Let's think over a snack," said Anna. She, Kristoff, and Elsa went to the kitchen. But Olaf had a different idea. He wandered off and went to the place where he knew he could always get answers: the library.

When Anna, Elsa, and Kristoff finished their snack, they realized Olaf had disappeared!

"Where did he go?" asked Elsa. They knew it wasn't like him to miss a minute of game night.

"I've got it!" said Kristoff. "He's playing hide-and-seek."

"Oooh!" Anna said. "We haven't played that in forever!"

"Ready or not, here we come!" called Anna.

They began searching through the dark, quiet castle, looking for the little snowman. The floors creaked, and shadows appeared on the walls. Playing hide-and-seek at night was eerie and fun! They peered around corners, behind doors, and under furniture. There were so many places to look.

Then something strange happened: Elsa went missing. Anna and Kristoff decided to split up and continue searching the castle, for Olaf *and* Elsa.

Suddenly, Anna paused. It was oddly quiet and still. Anna darted around, looking for Kristoff, and discovered he had vanished, too!

She felt a rush of excitement as she walked through the library, wondering where her friends were hiding.

Anna slowly opened a small cabinet door, and . . .

. . . found everyone stuffed inside! They laughed as stacks of books poured out of the cabinet.

"Olaf, you rearranged hide-and-seek!" Anna said with a chuckle. "Everyone had to find you! What a fun new game."

"I couldn't have done it without the help of these guys," Olaf said, smiling at his stack of books. "Books are so delightfully distracting."

"I'll hide this time," said Anna. "You guys count." Elsa and Kristoff climbed out, ready to play Olaf's reverse hide-and-seek again.

"Oh! I can hide again!" said Olaf as he snuggled down and buried his nose deeper in his book. "I still have one chapter left."

Mickey and the Kitten-Sitters

"Guess what?" Mickey Mouse said to his nephews, Morty and Ferdie. "We're going to watch Minnie's kitten, Figaro, while she visits her cousin. Isn't that exciting?"

Before Morty and Ferdie could answer, they heard wild clucking, flapping, and crowing coming from next door. Suddenly, Pluto raced across the lawn. A big, angry rooster followed close behind him.

"Pluto!" Minnie scolded. "Chasing chickens again! Aren't you ashamed?"

Pluto *was* a bit ashamed, but only because he had let the rooster bully him.

Mickey picked up Figaro. They were going to have such a fun night! Mickey waved goodbye to Minnie. Figaro meowed.

"It's a good thing Figaro is staying with you," Minnie told Mickey as she got into her car. "Maybe he can teach Pluto how to behave!"

Minnie was hardly out of sight when Figaro leapt out of Mickey's arms and scampered into the kitchen. With one quick hop, he jumped onto the table and knocked over a pitcher of cream.

Pluto growled at the kitten, but Mickey just cleaned up the mess.

"Take it easy, Pluto," he said. "Figaro is our guest."

At dinnertime, Pluto ate his food the way a good dog should. But no matter how hard Mickey and the boys tried, Figaro wouldn't touch the special food Minnie had left for him.

At bedtime, Figaro would not use the cushion Minnie had brought for him. Instead, he got into bed with Ferdie and tickled his ears. Finally, he bounced off to the kitchen.

"Uncle Mickey," called Morty, "did you remember to close the kitchen window?"

"Oh, no!" cried Mickey, jumping out of bed. The kitchen window was open, and Figaro was nowhere to be seen.

Mickey and the boys searched the entire house. They looked upstairs and downstairs, under every chair, and even in the yard. But they couldn't find the little kitten anywhere.

"You two stay here," Mickey told his nephews. "Pluto and I will find Figaro."

Mickey and Pluto went to Minnie's house first, but Figaro wasn't there. Next they went to the park down the street.

"Have you seen a little black-and-white kitten?" Mickey asked a policeman.

"I certainly have!" answered the policeman. "He was teasing the ducks by the pond!"

Mickey and Pluto hurried to the pond. Figaro wasn't there, but they *did* find some small, muddy footprints.

Mickey and Pluto followed the trail of footprints to Main Street, where they met a grocery truck driver.

"Have you seen a kitten?" Mickey asked.

"Have I!" cried the driver. "He knocked over my eggs!"

Mickey groaned as he paid for the eggs. Where was Figaro?

Mickey and Pluto searched the whole town, but there was no sign of the kitten. By the time they returned home, the sun was starting to rise.

Soon Minnie drove up. "Where is Figaro?" she asked.

No one answered.

"Something has happened to him!" Minnie cried. "Can't I trust you to watch *one* sweet little kitten?"

Just then, there was a loud clucking from the yard next door. A dozen frantic hens came flapping over the fence, with Figaro close behind.

"There's your sweet little kitten!" exclaimed Mickey. "He ran away last night and teased the ducks in the park. Then he broke the eggs in the grocery truck, and—"

"And now he's chasing chickens!" Minnie finished.

"I had hoped Figaro would teach Pluto some manners," Minnie said. "Instead, Pluto has been teaching him to misbehave!"

"Pluto didn't do anything wrong," Ferdie said.

But Minnie wouldn't listen. She picked up Figaro and quickly drove away.

"Don't worry, boys," said Mickey. "We'll tell her the whole story later, when she's not so upset."

"Please don't tell her too soon," begged Morty. "As long as Aunt Minnie thinks Pluto is a bad dog, we won't have to kitten-sit Figaro."

Mickey smiled and said, "Maybe we *should* wait a little while. We could all use some peace and quiet." And with that, he and Pluto settled down for a well-deserved nap.

Scamp the Hero

"Be careful, Scamp!" Lady called as she watched her son dash across the yard. "Don't bounce the ball too hard."

Lady, Tramp, and their four puppies were playing together outside their home. Scamp, the only boy puppy, was just like his father—always looking for an adventure!

After they finished playing ball, Scamp asked to visit the park by himself.

"All right," Tramp told his son. "But be careful."

"I will!" promised Scamp.

Scamp bounded out past the fence and onto the sidewalk. There was so much to see beyond his yard! He stopped to watch cars that were honking and beeping at one another.

He thought about chasing them, but he remembered his promise to his father. Scamp was determined to not get into any trouble.

But it wasn't long before trouble found him! Scamp passed an alley where a pack of big dogs were snarling at a little white poodle. The frightened puppy was backed up against a fence. She couldn't escape!

"Stay away from me!" the little poodle cried.

Scamp knew he had to help. He certainly couldn't fight the other dogs, but how else could he scare them away?

Then Scamp had an idea. He carefully crept behind a trash can and pushed it over. *CLANG! CLUNK! CRASH!*

The noise frightened the big dogs away. His trick had worked! Unfortunately, he also made a big mess. Garbage was everywhere.

But Scamp was more worried about the fluffy white poodle. "Don't be frightened," he told her. "I'm friendly."

"My name is Princess," the poodle said, "and you're my hero!"

Scamp liked being someone's hero!

"Why were those dogs bothering you?" asked Scamp.

"Because they wanted this," said Princess. She pulled something out from behind a box.

"Wow!" exclaimed Scamp. It was the biggest bone he'd ever seen.

Princess offered to share the bone with Scamp. But before they could start chewing on it, two police officers walked down the alley. Scamp and Princess quickly hid.

Scamp noticed the officers pointing to the garbage can he had tipped over. *Uh-oh*, he thought. Scamp was worried he would be taken to the pound if they caught him. Then his parents would never let him go out on his own again.

"Let's get out of here!" Scamp whispered to Princess.

The two puppies bolted away as the policemen examined the messy alleyway.

Scamp and Princess raced down a hill and into the park. But all that running had made the puppies very thirsty! Scamp hid the bone beneath a few leaves. "Let's get a drink of water before we have this," he suggested. "It will be safe here."

But when they got back, Scamp saw that a gardener had raked the bone into a big pile of leaves!

Scamp sprang into action. He dove straight into the leaves to get the bone back.

"Hey, stop that!" yelled the gardener.

Before the gardener could catch him, Scamp grabbed the bone. He and Princess ran away once again, scattering leaves everywhere. Scamp sure was getting into a lot of trouble!

Just then, Princess spotted a stern-looking police dog. He seemed to be searching for something.

"Maybe he's looking for us because of all the trouble I've caused," Scamp said. He thought about running away again, but then he remembered his promise to his parents. He knew what he had to do.

Scamp bravely stepped toward the police dog, carrying the giant bone. "What's going on here?" the police dog asked.

"I made the mess in the alley and scattered the gardener's pile of leaves," Scamp said.

But the police dog wasn't listening to Scamp. He was inspecting every inch of Princess's bone. "Yes, I think this is it," he announced.

"What?" Scamp asked.

"Let me explain," said the police dog. "Last night, there was a robbery at the museum."

"What did the thief take?" asked Scamp.

"A giant bone from our dinosaur skeleton," answered the police dog. He looked seriously at Scamp and Princess. "That bone was exactly like this one. Where did you get it?"

"I didn't steal it!" Princess exclaimed. "I found it in an alley."

"Maybe the real thief hid the bone there," suggested Scamp.

The police dog thought Scamp might be right. "Come with me," he said.

Meanwhile, Lady and Tramp were out looking for Scamp. He had been gone for a long time, and they couldn't find him anywhere.

They searched the park . . . but Scamp wasn't there!

Then they went to the pond where Scamp loved to chase the ducks . . . but Scamp wasn't there.

They even went to Tony's restaurant . . . but Scamp wasn't there, either! Lady and Tramp were starting to get very worried.

Finally, as they were walking along Main Street, they heard
someone shout, "Scamp. Look over here!"

Tramp froze in his tracks. He saw a crowd of excited people at the
museum down the street. The pair ran inside, hoping to find their son.

Lady and Tramp saw Scamp right away. Photographers were taking pictures of him and a white puppy!

"What's going on here?" Tramp asked Lady.

"I don't know," Lady replied, "but I'm just happy that Scamp is all right!"

When Scamp noticed his parents, he and Princess ran over to them.

"I'm sorry I didn't come straight home," Scamp told them. "But we had to help the police solve a robbery."

"Your son's a hero!" said Princess.

Tramp grinned. "That's my boy!"

"Princess was the one who found the stolen bone," Scamp said. He wasn't used to so much attention!

The director of the museum cleared his throat to make an announcement. "To thank our little heroes, we've prepared a feast." He pointed to a long table covered in treats for the puppies.

Scamp licked his lips. He had never seen so much delicious food all at once. And there were stacks of bones for him and Princess to enjoy—even if they weren't from a dinosaur!

The Best-Friend Sleepover

Tiana and Charlotte had been best friends for as long as they could remember. The two shared an unlikely friendship. While Charlotte was a big dreamer, Tiana knew the importance of hard work. But the two loved spending as much time together as they could.

"Come on, Tia. It's one day!" Charlotte said. "Surely you can be away from the restaurant for one day!"

Tiana sighed. For days Charlotte had been trying to talk her into going on a shopping trip. The problem was Tiana just had too much to do at her restaurant. She barely had time to sit down, much less take a whole day off.

"Please! Pretty please! With powdered sugar on top?" Charlotte pleaded.

Tiana looked around the kitchen. She still had to finish the gumbo, make the corn bread, and prepare that night's special dish.

"I'm sorry, Lottie," she said, shaking her head. "Tiana's Palace needs me. I don't have time to watch you try on a hundred dresses. Making sure everything here runs smoothly is just too important."

Tiana turned and went back to chopping carrots. "Maybe next week," she said. "Or the week after that."

Charlotte crossed her arms and pouted. "All you think about is your restaurant," she said. "What about your friends? This is *important*! I need a new dress for Big Daddy's gala."

"Lottie," Tiana began, "I told you—"

"Fine!" Charlotte said, cutting her off. "If that's how you feel, I'll go by myself. But see if I'm around the next time *you* need help!"

With a stomp, Charlotte turned around and stormed out of the kitchen, slamming the door behind her on the way out.

That afternoon, Charlotte went to her favorite boutique. She tried on every dress they had.

But shopping for a dress wasn't the same without her best friend. With no one to model for, Charlotte's favorite pastime just wasn't any *fun*.

Meanwhile, Tiana finished making the gumbo. And she made the corn bread. And she prepared the night's special.

Tiana looked at the pile of dirty dishes and sighed. Dishes were her least favorite part of working in the kitchen. But most nights she had Lottie to talk to while she worked. Listening to her best friend's excited chatter always seemed to make the cleanup go faster. Without her, the job dragged on and on.

That night, as Tiana got ready for bed, she looked out the window. If she had learned anything from her father, it was the importance of friends and family.

Tiana sighed. The restaurant was important, but not as important as Lottie. She knew she had to find a way to make up with her best friend.

Over at the LaBouff estate, Charlotte grumbled. And she complained. But most of all, she missed Tiana. Maybe she had taken things too far when she stormed out of Tiana's Palace. After all, the restaurant had been Tiana's dream for as long as Charlotte could remember. And making sure it ran smoothly *was* important.

Lottie knew she had to find a way to make up with her best friend.

The next morning, Tiana heard a noise coming
from the kitchen. Then she smelled something burning!
Flinging open the door, she found Charlotte standing over
a pot of boiling oil and burned beignets.

"Lottie!" Tiana said. "What are you doing?"

Just then, Tiana noticed a tear sliding down Charlotte's cheek.

"I just wanted to help," Charlotte explained. "I felt bad about yesterday, and I thought maybe I could make it up to you. But now I've ruined everything!"

Tiana sighed and hugged Charlotte. "I'm sorry, too. I should have remembered that some things are more important than my restaurant. And you're right at the top of that list!"

Tiana looked around the kitchen. "You were right, Lottie," she continued. "This place can run without me for a day. And I know just what we need. A good old-fashioned Tiana-and-Charlotte day!"

"Oh, Tia, really?" Charlotte asked. "That sounds wonderful!"

Tiana and Charlotte cleaned up the mess in the kitchen. Then Tiana showed her best friend how to make beignets—the right way.

In no time, Charlotte was rolling out the dough and frying up perfect beignets. "Now that's more like it!" she cried, examining her handiwork.

Next the two went shopping. Charlotte tried on dress after dress.
All the gowns that had seemed drab and boring the day before seemed
perfect now.

Soon Charlotte had found not one, not two, but *three* dresses for Big
Daddy's gala!

She even helped Tiana pick out the perfect gown.

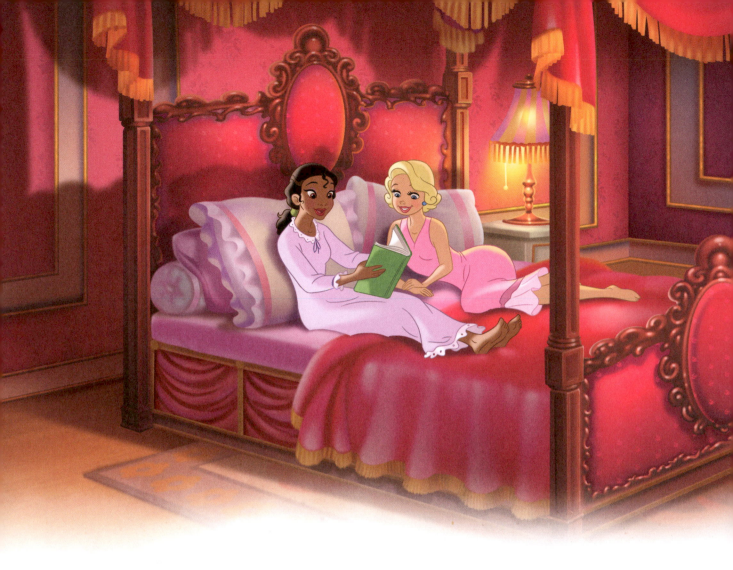

That night, Tiana lay on Charlotte's bed. "What are you doing, Lottie?" she called to her best friend. "I'm exhausted. Let's go to bed!"

"I'm looking for . . ." Charlotte began, then trailed off. "Where is it? Ah!" Charlotte poked her head out of the closet. "This!" she said, holding up a book.

Tiana smiled. It was the book her mother had read to them as children. "What a perfect way to end our day," she said.

Charlotte nodded and scrambled onto the bed next to Tiana. Tiana opened the book, and the two snuggled up to read the bedtime story together.

Power Outage!

Vanellope von Schweetz had missed her friend Wreck-It Ralph. He spent most of his time in *Fix-It Felix, Jr.*—the game where he lived. But they were planning to meet back at the arcade for some best friend fun!

It was the end of the day at the arcade, and the video game characters were gathering in Game Central Station. Suddenly, all the lights in the station went out. It was a power outage!

"I think we're stuck," Ralph told Vanellope. He was right. Until the power came back on, no one was going anywhere!

"Don't worry, everyone!" Fix-It Felix, Jr., called out. "My trusty hammer and I will have this fixed in no time!"

Ralph and Vanellope started to make their way toward Felix, but it was hard to see without the lights.

"Come on, stink brain," Vanellope said. "I think I see a—*aaah!*" Vanellope had run into someone!

"Oh! I'm s-sorry, Vanellope! I d-didn't see you there." It was Gene, the Nicelander mayor from the *Fix-It Felix, Jr.* game.

"D-do you think the power will be out f-for a long time?" he asked.

"I hope so!" Vanellope said. "This is fun!"

Vanellope started bouncing excitedly, but she stopped when she saw how nervous Gene was. "What's wrong?" Vanellope asked him.

"The truth is," Gene said, "the idea of spending the night away from home scares me!"

Just then, Felix ran past with his hammer. "Felix, tap Gene with your hammer!" Ralph suggested. "Maybe then he won't be scared anymore."

Felix hit Gene lightly with his hammer. It was supposed to fix anything. The friends waited and waited, but nothing happened. Gene was still scared.

"Sorry, Gene," Felix said sadly. "I guess there are just some things my hammer can't fix."

Vanellope and Ralph knew they needed to find a way to distract Gene until Felix could get the power back on.

"Are you thinking what I'm thinking, kid?" Ralph whispered to Vanellope.

"Absolutely!" Vanellope said. "Party! Come on, everyone! We're going to have a slumber party!"

"Wait, what? No!" Ralph said. He had definitely *not* been thinking about throwing a party.

"Trust me, big guy," Vanellope said, patting Ralph on the back. "I know what I'm doing." Then she climbed onto Ralph's shoulders and yelled, "Now let's have some fun!"

Ralph sighed. If there was one thing he knew about Vanellope, it was that once she got an idea in her head, there was no changing her mind.

Ralph looked around. "Satine," he called out, recognizing a fellow member of his Bad Guy support group, Bad-Anon. "Think you can help us out with some light?"

"It would be my pleasure," Satine said. He lit his staff, and a small circle of light filled the room.

The video game characters wasted no time in following Vanellope's lead. Soon they were all happily playing party games.

"Who knew that Zombie would be so good at this?" Ralph said, watching Zombie bob for apples.

But Gene wasn't paying any attention to Ralph. He was too busy wishing he was safe in his own bed.

"Come on, Gene," Ralph said, pushing his friend toward a limbo line. "You should give it a try!"

Gene took a deep breath and limboed under the pole. He could really bend!

"How's it going, Felix?" Ralph called to his friend.

Ralph looked around. Where *was* Felix?

"Up here, Ralph!" Felix called from within one of the ceiling vents high above Ralph. "Can't talk now! I think I'm getting close!"

Gene was having fun, but he was still worried. Vanellope needed another idea.

"It's time for charades!" she cried. "Gene, you keep time. Ralph, you're up first!"

"I don't know about this," Ralph and Gene said at the same time. Gene thought he'd be too scared to keep time, and Ralph didn't think he'd be very good at charades. But Vanellope wouldn't take no for an answer.

"Rooster? No. Ice cream? No. Giraffe? No. I got it, I got it, I got it. *Lollipop?*" Vanellope yelled as Ralph tried to act out the first word.

"Time's up!" Gene yelled.

"It's a cy-bug! I was trying to be a cy-bug!" Ralph explained.

Vanellope could see that Gene was starting to feel better. And she planned to keep it that way! She grabbed Gene by the arm and dragged him toward the starting line for a three-legged race.

Gene glanced at Vanellope's fellow *Sugar Rush* racers. They looked tough. "Vanellope—maybe this isn't a good idea," he said.

"Come *on*, Gene. We have to beat Taffyta and Candlehead!" Vanellope replied as she tied her leg to Gene's.

Vanellope was very competitive, and she wasn't going to lose this race.

Before Gene could say another word, Sour Bill waved the starting flag. The racers were off!

Taffyta and Candlehead quickly took the lead, with Wyntchell and Duncan from the Donut Police close behind.

"*Vanellope!*" Gene cried as he tried to keep up with her. "Slow down!"

"You slow down, you lose," Vanellope said. "Come on, Gene. You can do it!"

Vanellope pulled Gene along as fast as she could, but they were still in third place.

Suddenly, one of the racers tripped! Everyone went flying—except for Vanellope and Gene. They raced into the lead and across the finish line in first place.

Vanellope jumped up and down. She was so excited they had won the race!

"You did it, Gene!" Ralph said, lifting Gene onto his shoulders.

"I did! I won!" Gene cheered loudly.

"Well, *we* won. But you were great!" Vanellope said.

Gene was so proud of himself. He had gotten over his fear and had so much fun doing it. He knew he couldn't have done it without the help of his friends Ralph and Vanellope.

"And look, you made it through the night!" Ralph said. He was right. The sun had come out! Suddenly, with a bang, Game Central Station lit up. Felix had fixed the power.

"I never thought I would make it through a whole night away from home," Gene said. "But now that I have, I guess it's not so scary after all. Thanks, guys!"

"Of course, buddy," Ralph said. "What are friends for?"

Who Cares? Pooh Cares!

One bright and cheery day in the Hundred-Acre Wood, a mama duck waited patiently for her eggs to hatch.

Suddenly . . . *crack, crack, crack*! Three fuzzy yellow ducklings poked through their spotted shells.

Mama Duck greeted them with a loud and proud "Quaaaack!"

She then led her ducklings to the pond for their first swimming lesson.

But Mama Duck did not know that one spotted egg was left behind. Beneath a pile of soft green leaves, another fuzzy yellow head poked out from a shell. The tiny duckling began to quack softly for his mama. But there was no answer. He did not know what to do, so he sat and waited . . . and waited . . . and waited.

On this very same day in the Hundred-Acre Wood, Winnie the Pooh and his best friend, Piglet, decided to go for a morning stroll.

It wasn't long before Piglet's ears perked up. "Pooh," he said. "Do you hear something?"

Pooh listened carefully. "I believe I do," he answered. "It sounds like flapping and rustling and . . . quacking!"

Pooh parted some lilies to discover a tiny fuzzy duckling sitting there.

"We must find his mother!" said Pooh.

So the two friends gently nudged the duckling out of his nest and went off to search. But there were no ducks in sight.

"There's only one thing to do now," said Pooh. "We shall take him to my house."

"Before we do," said Piglet, "this little duckling needs a name."

"Oh, yes," Pooh agreed. "And I think you just named him."

"I did?" asked Piglet. "Funny, I don't remember . . ."

"Little," said Pooh. "That's what we'll call him. Because he is so very that!"

"Follow us, Little!" said Piglet with a giggle. "We are taking you to Pooh's house."

At Pooh's house, the friends found a small box to make into a comfy bed for Little.

Pooh let the duckling borrow a blanket so he'd be nice and cozy, and Piglet set up a night-light in case he was afraid of the dark.

Then Piglet filled a saucer with water and left it next to Little's new bed. "Just in case he gets thirsty," he said.

The next morning, Pooh, Piglet, and Little went to visit Rabbit for their first meal of the day.

"We were wondering if you might have a little something for him to eat," Pooh said.

Exactly one minute later, Rabbit presented Little with a plate of tiny green beans, peas, and half a chopped tomato.

"Oh, look!" cried Piglet, watching Little nibble away. "He likes it!"

"Of course," Rabbit said. "What would you expect!"

"I would expect you might have a little something for us, as well, please," said Pooh.

Rabbit returned a minute later with some honey.

After breakfast, Pooh and Piglet took Little to Kanga and Roo's house.

"Oh, boy, Mama," said Roo. "I have a new friend! I'm going to teach him all my games!" The first game was follow-the-leader.

After a while, Roo moved on to playing hide-and-seek.

Soon after, Little was in for something special. For there was nothing Roo loved more than making pies from soft, squishy mud.

After a bath and a snack, Pooh, Piglet, and Little headed home and stopped to visit Owl on the way.

"Well, bust my beak, aren't you something!" pronounced Owl. "Let me show you how to primp and plump those fuzzy yellow feathers of yours, dear fellow!" Owl proceeded to fuss with his feathers. When Little tried to imitate him, the duckling puffed up two sizes!

After saying goodbye and thanking Owl, a fuller, fluffier Little waddled home with Winnie the Pooh.

The very next day, Tigger
and Roo came to Pooh's
house to give Little a
bouncing lesson.

"Hoo-hoo-hoo!" cried Tigger. "Let's bounce to the
pond and take you for a swim, li'l Little!"

So Little got his first lesson in bouncing, which, for him,
was more like a long waddle followed by two quick hops.

At the pond, Roo introduced Little to the most amazing creatures!

Little took a ride on the back of a turtle, splashed with a playful perch, and bounced with a croaking frog.

"I think he likes it here," said Roo.
After their swim, Tigger bounced Roo and Little home.

The next day, after a good night's sleep, Eeyore came by to show Little his home and to ask Little if he could teach him how to waddle.

Little nodded willingly and began to waddle around the thistle patch. Then Eeyore began to waddle, too! He waddled up; he waddled back; he waddled left; he waddled right . . . then he tipped right over!

"I knew it was too good to last," said Eeyore.

When it was time to leave, Eeyore walked Little to Pooh's house. But before long, he realized they were lost.

"Better just sit tight and wait for somebody to come and find us," Eeyore said.

Eeyore and Little nestled together and took a little nap while they waited to be found. After what seemed like a very long while, Pooh and Piglet found them fast asleep beneath a willow tree.

Together, the friends walked and waddled home to Pooh's house.

When Pooh and Piglet put Little to bed, they heard the duckling quacking in his sleep.

"Listen, Pooh," said Piglet. "I think he's quacking, 'Maaa-maaaa, Maaa-maaa.'"

"Oh, dear," said Pooh. "Perhaps it's time to try to find Little's mother again."

The next day, with Kanga and Roo's help, Pooh and Piglet found Mama Duck! After quite a lot of talking and clapping and quacking, they managed to explain what had happened.

Soon everyone had gathered at the duck pond.
And there followed a heartwarming reunion
between Little and his mama.

When Mulan arrived at the Imperial Palace, she gasped with delight at the sight. "It's even more breathtaking than I remember," said Mulan.

"Don't stand there and gape all afternoon. We are on a tight schedule. It would do you well to be prompt for tonight's performance," Chi Fu said, frowning.

Chi Fu led Mulan through the maze of palace hallways before settling on a door. "You may prepare for the evening's festivities here in the Common Room," said Chi Fu. "And please, Mulan, do not disrespect the Emperor with your tendency for tardiness and turmoil."

"Tardiness! Turmoil! Ha!" exclaimed Mulan as the imperial attendants pinned up her hair. "It's as if Chi Fu doesn't even know me. Tonight I will bring honor to my family by being intelligent, elegant, and graceful."

But just as Mulan spoke, Cri-Kee sprang from his cage. He skittered across the room and scooted out the door.

Mulan dashed down the hall and into the music room in search of her mischievous travel companion. Much to Mulan's delight, the playful notes of the pi-pa and paixiao filled the chamber.

But her delight quickly turned into dismay. Cri-Kee had climbed up a musician's sleeve. Mulan wondered how she was going to catch the cricket without causing a disturbance.

I could dance my way across the floor toward the cricket, Mulan thought. She swayed and spun to the music. But just as she reached Cri-Kee, he jumped from the pi-pa to the paixiao, then sped down the palace stairs.

Cri-Kee darted into the Imperial Study, where the Emperor composed all his official correspondence.

It will bring shame to the Fa name if my cricket disturbs such serene surroundings, thought Mulan.

She lunged for Cri-Kee as he hopped across the writing table, leaving overturned brushes and upended inkstones in his wake. The clever cricket made a clean escape, but Mulan's dress did not.

Mulan chased Cri-Kee into the Imperial War Room and looked around for a moment in reverence. Having served in the Imperial Army, Mulan understood the importance of that place. It was there that the Emperor and his generals strategized their battle plans. Mulan panicked as Cri-Kee scampered across the hand-drawn maps and flitted about the Emperor's banners.

Then she noticed a suit of armor in the cabinet. Thinking fast, Mulan grabbed the battle helmet, planning to use it to catch the impish cricket. She followed Cri-Kee down the hall and swung open the doors to . . .

The Imperial Theater!

The Emperor and his guests all turned to look at Mulan. "So much for grace, punctuality, and politeness," she muttered.

She had dishonored her
family in the presence of the
Emperor. And to make matters
worse, Cri-Kee had fled behind
the screen set up for the
shadow play.

But Mulan did not despair. She bowed to the Emperor, then marched toward the stage. Once behind the screen, Mulan leapt, lunged, and spun at Cri-Kee until she finally caught him. The Emperor's audience laughed, assuming this comical scene was part of the performance.

Pleased by Mulan's impromptu show, the Emperor gave her an encouraging smile. "The night star is most radiant when it is truest to itself," he mused.

Mulan considered the
Emperor's wise words. Her
adventures with Cri-
Kee had brought
pride, not shame,
to the Fa name.

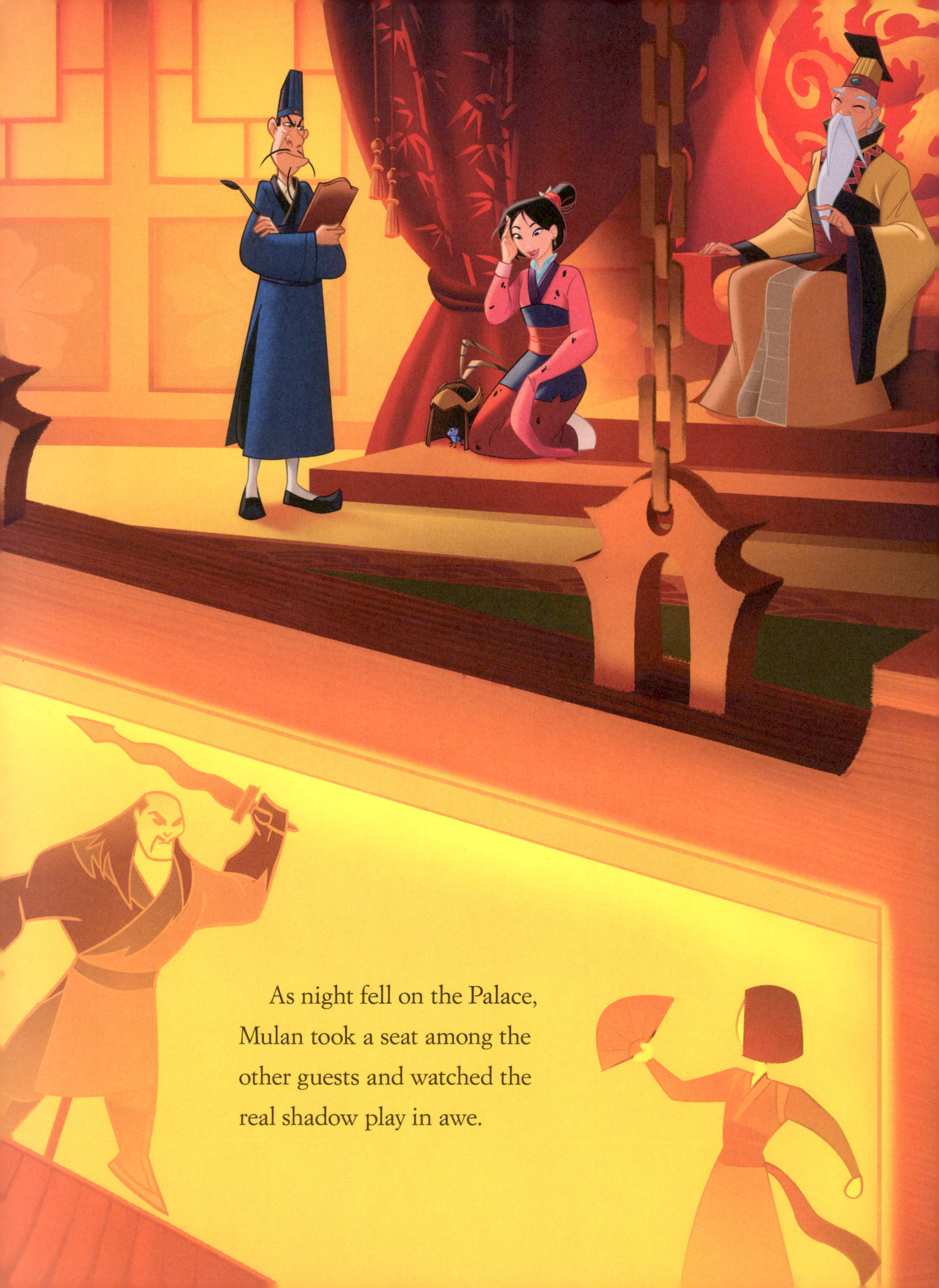

As night fell on the Palace, Mulan took a seat among the other guests and watched the real shadow play in awe.

Rally to the Finish!

German superstar racer Max Schnell had invited Lightning McQueen and some of the other World Grand Prix racers to the first-ever Black Forest Rally Race Invitational.

Lightning was thrilled! He happily accepted the invitation and asked Mater, Luigi, and Guido to go along with him as his race crew.

When Team Lightning arrived in Germany, they were greeted at the airport by Max. *"Willkommen!"* he said.

"Gesundheit," Mater said, testing out his German.

Mater had changed on the plane and couldn't wait to show off his outfit. "These here are genuine Materhosen," he told Max. "I can give you the name of my tailor if you'd like!"

Both Mater and Lightning were so excited to be exploring and racing in a new city. They knew this was going to be quite an adventure.

Team Lightning was soon whisked off to a prerace party. At the end of the evening, Lightning told Mater he wanted to head to the Black Forest to practice on the racetrack.

An old gentlecar overheard their plans. "Black Forest at night, eh? Just beware of that *Waldgeister* monster. It's the fastest, scariest monster in the forest."

"A m-m-monster?" said Mater. The old car chuckled and drove off.

"I'm sure that 'monster' is just an old legend," said Lightning as he and Mater drove to the forest.

"I hope yer right," said Mater, relaxing a little. Then he looked at all the surrounding trees. "This place sure is pretty!"

"Especially at top speed!" said Lightning as he revved his engine and took off.

"Whee-hoo!
This is fun!" yelled
Mater. "Last one
out of the forest is a
rusty tow hitch!"

Following the
racetrack, the two
best buddies drifted
down the fire road,
crossed over streams,
and cruised across
bridges until . . .

. . . they got lost. Lightning had gone in one direction, and Mater had accidentally driven off in another.

"Lightning? Lightning? Hellooooo?" yelled Mater. All Mater heard was the wind howling and the trees creaking.

Suddenly, he felt something brush against him.

"Who's there?" he gasped as he spun around.

A large shadowy figure loomed over him. "The Baldmeister monster! *AHHHHHH!*" Mater screamed as he took off backward. "He's gonna get me!"

Meanwhile, Lightning was driving through a different part of the forest. He heard the screaming and headed toward Mater. "Mater! I'm coming!" he yelled.

Once the two friends were reunited, they found the racetrack and
followed it out of the forest.

"The Baldtire monster is *real*," Mater said, shivering.

Lightning sighed. "Mater, you're just imagining things. That monster
is not real."

"He *is* real!" Mater insisted. "I ain't never going back in that forest
again!"

The next day was race day! Just before the race began, Mater yelled out to the racers, "You guys aren't still gonna race in the Black Forest, are you?"

"Why wouldn't we?" asked one of the cars.

"Because there's a monster that lives in there!" exclaimed Mater.

The other cars brushed off Mater's warning. After all, there was no such thing as monsters.

The green flag dropped—and the cars were off!

All of a sudden, the racers heard a low grumbling that shook the forest floor.

Then Lightning felt something brush his side and heard a creaking sound. "What was that?" he yelled.

The racers stopped in their tracks and looked at each other, panic-stricken.

"Maybe Mater was right," said Lightning.

All the racers took off! They sped down a rocky slope and skidded around turns. They saw shadows quickly creeping up behind them.

A ravine was just ahead of them. The racers didn't think twice. They raced forward at full speed and leapt over it!

Lightning and the other cars raced for their lives toward the finish line. The fans couldn't believe what they were seeing. All four racers crossed the finish line at the same moment, breaking the Rally Race record for the fastest time!

Lightning and the other racers drove up onto the winner's podium. They had all been awarded first place!

"What motivated all of you to race your best today?" asked a reporter.

"Well, we couldn't have done it without the *Waldgeister* monster," said Lightning.

Mater glanced back at the old gentlecar and gave him a wink.

The Birthday Wish

"Good night, my loves," Duchess said. Her tail swished softly as she gave each of her kittens—Berlioz, Toulouse, and Marie—a tender nuzzle.

"Sleep tight, kiddos," O'Malley said as he tucked them in.

Berlioz and Toulouse purred happily, but Marie didn't want to go to bed. "*Please* may I go to the party tonight?" she asked. "I promise to be very good!"

Duchess smiled and shook her head. "Scat Cat will have other birthday parties you can go to when you're older. For now, you need a good night's sleep."

Duchess and O'Malley left and shut the door quietly behind them.

Marie listened as Berlioz began to snore softly. Then Toulouse's whiskers began twitching. Soon both her brothers were fast asleep.

But Marie was wide awake.

Voices drifted from downstairs, then music. Duchess and O'Malley were throwing a birthday party for their friend Scat Cat. He was a jazz musician who had helped Duchess and the kittens when they were separated from their owner.

Marie sighed. Oh, how she wished she were allowed to join them! Why, Scat Cat was her friend, too. It wasn't fair! After all, Marie could laugh and dance and sing as well as any grown-up.

That's it! Marie thought. She could sneak into the party if she looked like an adult. Tiptoeing carefully, she made her way down the stairs. The coat closet would be full of things she could use to disguise herself!

The noise from the ballroom became louder as Marie slipped into the dark closet. She rummaged around, trying things on. The feather boa tickled her nose. The frilly bonnet wasn't glamorous enough for a party. The dark glasses made it impossible for Marie to see anything.

Finally, she found the perfect disguise. Marie thought she looked very grown-up.

Marie crept into the parlor and looked around. Scat Cat was leading the band in a fast-paced jazz number. Duchess and O'Malley were chatting with some cats in the corner. But most of the cats were dancing. They danced on the floor, on tables—there was even a cat swinging from the chandelier!

Marie wanted to dance, too. "But I have to stay quiet," she reminded herself. "I mustn't get caught!"

"This is a beautiful house," someone said. Marie turned around to see a lady cat wearing a sparkly collar. She was talking to Marie!

"Thank you," Marie said. Then she slapped a paw over her mouth. She was in disguise as a guest. No one could know this was her house!

"I mean," Marie added in a hurry, "I think so, too."

The lady cat gave Marie a funny look. Marie decided to change the subject, fast.

"I like your collar," she said.

"I like your hat," the cat said. Marie beamed. It was working! Her disguise was *perfect*.

Nearby, a cat in an apron appeared, carrying a large platter. "Who wants tuna ice cream?" he said.

"I do! I do!" Marie raised her paw and jumped up and down. Then she remembered—she was supposed to act like a grown-up!

The aproned cat handed her a bowl. "Thank you very much, young fellow," Marie said in her best adult voice. As she tasted the ice cream, she purred loudly. Tuna was her favorite!

Later, some of the guests played party games.
Marie enjoyed the charades, but Pin the Tail on
the Doggy was her favorite. She won every round!

As Marie removed her blindfold, the band started playing a new tune. Scat Cat put his trumpet down.

"You're on your own, fellas!" he said to the band. "This birthday cat has got a date with the dance floor." Scat Cat walked over to Marie. "Ma'am," he said with a wink, "may I have this dance?"

Marie forgot all about getting in trouble. She put her little paw in his, and Scat Cat led her out onto the dance floor.

"Enjoying the party, Marie?" Scat Cat asked.

"Oh, yes!" Marie replied. Then she gasped. "I mean . . . who's Marie?" she asked, trying to cover up her mistake.

"Don't worry. Your secret is safe with me," Scat Cat said. "Let's just dance!"

The music swelled, and Marie took Scat Cat's advice. She swayed, bopped, and jumped to the beat. Then, as the piano trilled, Scat Cat spun her around like a top. Marie whirled—and her disguise went flying off!

"Marie!"

The music stopped, and everyone stared. Marie's disguise was gone, and her mother was marching right toward her!

"Young lady, you are supposed to be in bed!" Duchess said.

Marie looked up sadly. "I'm sorry, Mama," she said. "I didn't mean to disappoint you." Marie felt terrible for making her mother angry.

"Hey now," said a rumbly voice. Marie looked up. It was Scat Cat!

"Say, Duchess, it *is* my birthday," Scat Cat said, "and Marie's my friend. How about letting her stay?" Scat Cat leaned toward the birthday cake on the table. "It's my birthday wish!" Then he blew out all the candles and winked at Marie. She smiled back.

Duchess sighed, looking closely at Marie and Scat Cat. "Well, just this once, I suppose. But you are going to bed early tomorrow night, Marie. Understood?"

Marie nodded happily. "Thank you, Mama! I promise I'll never sneak out again."

So Marie stayed at the party, singing and dancing and talking with the grown-ups. Finally, it was time for everyone to go home. Marie was as sleepy as she had ever been. As Duchess carried her up to bed, Marie heard Scat Cat call, "Thanks for coming to my party, Marie!"

"Happy birthday, Scat Cat!" Marie called back. "Thank you for the dance!"

Marie couldn't stop smiling as Duchess tucked her back into bed with her brothers. She would never forget her special night and Scat Cat's birthday wish!

Pajama Party

Wart couldn't sleep. Ever since Merlin the wizard had arrived, Wart's life had been turned upside down. Merlin insisted on turning Wart into difference animals to enhance Wart's educational experiences—and that was on top of all his normal chores. It was a lot to handle.

That night, the boy looked out his window and saw that the light in Merlin's rickety tower was still on.

Wart paid Merlin a visit. When he arrived, he found that
Merlin's owl, Archimedes, was even grumpier than normal.

"It's too drafty!" Archimedes said. "It's leaky. It smells weird!"

"Go to *sleep*, you wretched creature!" Merlin shouted.

"Sleep? In this unsuitable environment?" Archimedes huffed.

"I can't sleep, either," Wart said.

"Here," Merlin said, waving his wand. A gigantic book wafted toward Wart. "This one is very boring. Give it a read. It can be part of your bedtime routine."

"What's a bedtime routine?" Wart asked.

"Of course he doesn't have a bedtime routine," Merlin muttered to himself. "Who would've taught him?"

Just then, Merlin jumped up, suddenly energetic. "Since nobody is getting any sleep, we might as well have a party."

Archimedes eyed the wizard suspiciously.

Merlin waved his wand again, and

presto change-o . . .

. . . Wart was wearing pajamas! Having never had real pajamas before, he was delighted.

"What is the meaning of this?" Archimedes demanded. "Just because I'm wearing a hat with a tassel does not mean I'm going to bed."

"No, of course not," Merlin scoffed. "We're just having a party. A pajama party!"

"What do we do at a pajama party?" Wart asked.

"Usually there's a story," Merlin said, raising his wand again.

"Ribbitus-Rabbitus!" he shouted.

POOF!

Wart could tell something was different. He shook his head and felt a bit confused. His long ears flopped. Wait—long ears? "We're rabbits!" Wart exclaimed.

"The best storyteller in Britain is Mama Rabbit," Merlin explained. "Come on! We'll be late!"

Wart hopped after the wizard, and Archimedes kept pace above as they made their way into the woods.

Soon Merlin skidded to a stop. "We're here," he said, pointing to the entrance of a burrow.

"Archimedes," Merlin added, "I'm afraid you'll need to listen from a distance."

"Why?" Wart asked.

"It's part of the tension between predators and prey, my boy. You see, some owls eat rabbits. Our Archimedes wouldn't, of course. But it's safer for everyone if Archimedes stays here and isn't accidentally threatening."

Archimedes rolled his eyes.

Merlin and Wart squeezed themselves through a tunnel and eventually settled near the back of the burrow. The home was filled with young bunnies, all listening intently to Mama Rabbit. Merlin muttered a spell so that he and Wart could understand what she was saying.

Mama Rabbit's voice was gentle, and as she spoke, Wart could see the story unfolding.

All the young bunnies started to close their eyes and drift off to sleep.

"Those little bunnies found their way home," Mama Rabbit said, "and soon after, they fell fast asleep."

Wart yawned. "This is a very good story, don't you think so?" the boy whispered. Then a soft snore rumbled nearby. It was coming from Merlin.

"Ever since that day," Mama Rabbit said, her voice barely a whisper, "we bunnies have told the story of the—"

"Owl!" a bunny screamed.

Suddenly, everyone in the burrow was *very awake*. There, peeking out from behind his rabbit friends, was Archimedes.

"You didn't really expect me to wait outside, did you? I could barely hear the story," the owl confessed.

Merlin, Wart, and Archimedes started backing toward the exit of the burrow amid the bunnies' chaos. Archimedes knew he had made a mistake coming in here.

"Get out!" Mama Rabbit shrieked at the uninvited guests. Her bunnies quickly joined in.

"Merlin! Do something!" Wart cried.

Merlin was panicking a little, but he knew what to do.

FOOMP!

As the smoke cleared, Wart realized he was back in Merlin's tower. He touched his head. The long ears were gone. "I'm a boy again," Wart said.

"And we're back home," Archimedes added. "Not a moment too soon."

Merlin prepared a tray with a pitcher and three cups. "Here we go," he said, spinning around triumphantly. "Warm milk."

As the trio moved to the table, Wart found himself thinking about Mama Rabbit's story. He noticed how soft his new pajamas were. And he suddenly felt very dozy. "You know—" Wart began.

"Shhh," Merlin replied. He pointed at Archimedes, who had fallen asleep. Wart stifled a giggle.

Merlin carefully picked up the
slumbering bird. He settled Archimedes
in his birdhouse and drew a blanket over
his shoulders. "There," Merlin
said, patting Archimedes gently.

Wart stretched and yawned. He
was ready for bed, too.